Some Cat!

Mary
Casanova

Pictures by
Ard Hoyt

Farrar Straus Giroux
New York

For Kate and Chris—and their adopted cats
—M.C.

For Grandma Deborah Hansen, with love
—A.H.

Text copyright © 2012 by Mary Casanova
Pictures copyright © 2012 by Ard Hoyt
Distributed in Canada by D&M Publishers, Inc.
Color separations by Embassy Graphics
Printed in China by Macmillan Production (Asia) Ltd.,
Kwun Tong, Kowloon, Hong Kong (supplier code 10)
Designed by Jay Colvin
First edition, 2012
1 3 5 7 9 10 8 6 4 2

mackids.com

Library of Congress Cataloging-in-Publication Data
Casanova, Mary.
   Some cat! / Mary Casanova ; pictures by Ard Hoyt. — 1st ed.
       p.   cm.
   Summary: When Violet the cat is adopted she has trouble sharing her new
kingdom with the family dogs until they save her from some home invaders.
   ISBN: 978-0-374-37123-4
   [1. Cats—Fiction.   2. Dogs—Fiction.]   I. Hoyt, Ard, ill.   II. Title.

PZ7.C266Sn 2012
[E]—dc22
                                                      2010021744

Day after day, Violet sat in a cage.

She'd once had a home—with too little food and too much shouting—but she no longer cared to remember it.

Violet knew she was meant for more. She was meant to rule a kingdom, with sharp claws and velvet paws.

When anyone stopped by, she arched her royal fur. *"Meowwww! Hisssss! Spat!"*

"That's some cat," people would say. To Violet's dismay, they often chose a tiny kitten—*purr, purr, purr*—and went away.

Until one morning, a man and woman stopped by.
Violet growled and yowled. *"Meowwww! Hissss! Spat!"*
She arched her royal fur.

But the couple didn't back away.

Finally, Violet lay down on her royal bed.

"She needs a home," said the woman.

"Let's give her a chance," said the man.

The moment Violet stepped into the house, two dogs bounded at her.

"*Meowwww! Hissss! Spat!*" She swiped at the dogs with her sharp royal claws.

Zippity ran in circles. *"Ya-yippity, yappity, yeep-yeep-yeep!"*

George flopped down. *"Wa-roooo! Wa-roo-roo-roo-roo!"*

Now, whenever the two dogs came near, Violet howled and yowled.

At dinner, Violet scowled and growled—and always ate first.

When Zippity played with his favorite toy, Violet swept toward him like a sidewinder snake. *"Meowwww! Hisssss! Spat!"*

When he zipped away—*Ya-yippity, yappity, yeep-yeep-yeep!*—Violet claimed the toy for herself.

When George tried to rest, Violet claimed the hammock as her own.

"*Wa-rooo!*" George said.

"*Wa-roo-roo-roo-roo!*"

"Think she'll work out?" asked the woman.

"Hope so," said the man.

When George and Zippity went fishing, Violet stayed behind, content with a little quiet.

She surveyed her kingdom. She caught mice.

And then she stretched out in the sun for a good, long nap.

But one afternoon, Violet woke with a start. She sprang to her velvet paws.

A chorus of barking drew near.

"Ga-roof!"

"Roe-roe-roe!"

"Woof! Woof! Woof!"

Violet ran for the nearest tree, but the stray dogs blocked her path.

She arched her royal fur.

"Meowwww! Hisssss! Spat!"

But the dogs didn't back away. Instead, they chased Violet—up and down, in and out, over and under, through and around—until—

Violet raced for the woodpile!

"Ga-roof!"

"Roe-roe-roe!"

"Woof! Woof! Woof!"

The strange dogs barked and pawed. They snorted and clawed, until—

the woodpile tumbled. Kersplat!

Violet YOWLED!

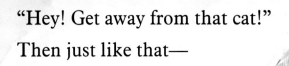

"Hey! Get away from that cat!"
Then just like that—

George and Zippity bounded to shore.

"Wa-roooo! Wa-roo-roo-roo-roo!"

"Ya-yippity-yappity-yeep-yeep-yeep!"

George and Zippity arched their doggy fur. They snarled and growled, they yapped and howled, until—

the other dogs fled, tails down.

Violet shivered. *"Meow."*

Violet quivered. *"Yeow."*

Then, with her deepest bow of thanks, she rolled on her back and allowed George and Zippity to rest nearby.

"Wow," said the woman.

"Amazing," said the man.

After that, Violet found life a little easier. When she caught mice, she often let them go free.

When Zippity wanted to play, Violet sometimes let him win.

When George lay in his hammock, Violet contentedly surveyed her kingdom below.

And when they all went fishing, Violet joined in, perched on the royal prow.

"That's some cat," the woman said.

"*Our* cat," said the man.

And most nights, Violet didn't mind sharing. She tucked away her claws, and ruled her kingdom with endless purring—*purr, purr, purr*—

and soft velvet paws.